Pedal Power

"Can't catch me!"
Connor cycled through the park at top speed. Greg and Amaya rode along behind him.

"SCREECH!"

Everyone stopped. There was something on the ground.
"It's a car steering wheel," said Amaya. "What's it doing here?"
"Look!" called Connor. "There's a tyre and a mirror, too."

The friends followed the trail of scrap metal. It led to a tottering tower of cars! Connor, Amaya and Greg bumped fists.

PJ MASKS ARE ON THEIR WAY, INTO THE NIGHT TO SAVE THE DAY!

CATBOY!

GREG BECOMES . . . GEKKO!

The PJ Masks had to find out what was going on.
Catboy touched the PJ Picture Player screen.
"Let's take the Cat-Car and go back to the park," he decided.
Catboy was in for a shock. The Cat-Car had disappeared!
The Gekko-Mobile and the Owl Glider were gone, too.

"How can we be heroes without vehicles?" groaned Catboy.
"We'll have to use our bikes," said Gekko.
The PJ Masks pedalled into the night.

The park was full of stacked cars. Romeo waved down from his Lab.
"My Cat-Car!" cried Catboy.
The baddie had stolen the PJ Masks' super vehicles! The Cat-Car, the Gekko-Mobile and the Owl Glider were trapped underneath a massive electromagnet.

"You can't steal our super vehicles!"
shouted Owlette.
"I'll only keep the best one," simpered Romeo,
"then I'll squash the others flat!"

Romeo jumped in the Owl Glider.
"Quick!" shouted Owlette. "After him!"
Catboy shook his head. He wanted to
get his Cat-Car down first.
"We've got to use our bikes," said Gekko.
"Romeo is getting away!"

The PJ Masks pedalled after the Owl Glider. Owlette flew up to try and lure Romeo down to the ground. Suddenly Catboy put on the brakes.

This bike will **never** catch Romeo! I'm going back to get the Cat–Car.

Owlette caught up with the Owl Glider.
"Land now, Romeo!" she cried.
"Think you can catch me on your bike?" scoffed the baddie. "Forget it, birdie!"

Romeo chased Owlette across the sky. At last she managed to lure the Owl Glider down onto the street – ready for the other PJ Masks to snatch it back.

"Catboy! Gekko! NOW!"

But Catboy had gone. Gekko tried to save the Owl Glider on his own, but it was much too big for one hero to catch. Romeo flew away.

Owlette and Gekko rode back to the park.
"Catboy!" said Owlette. "We could have used some help there."
"I was going to help," insisted Catboy, "in my amazing Cat-Car."

There was no time to argue. Romeo was swooping down in the
Owl Glider! The baddie jumped out and marched up to his Lab.
"Eeny meeny, miny, mo . . . which one is the next to go?"
Romeo pressed a button to release another super vehicle.
Gekko gasped. "My Gekko-Mobile!"

The PJ Masks cycled after Romeo.

"We'll get him this time!" said Gekko.

Owlette turned a corner. She came head-to-head with the Gekko-Mobile.

"PJ Masks again?" sighed Romeo. "You're starting to bore me."

Romeo blasted Owlette with water spray.

"WHOOSH!"

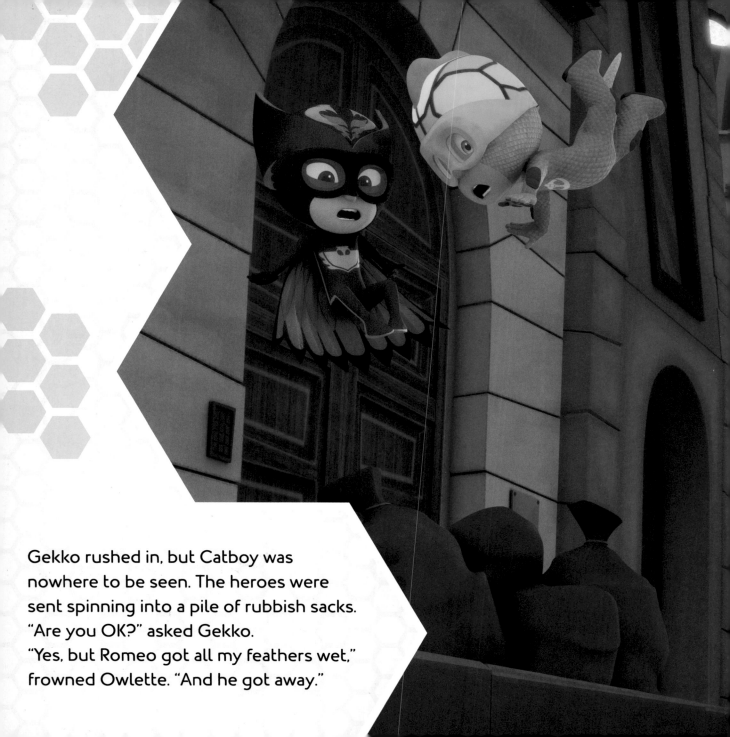

Gekko rushed in, but Catboy was nowhere to be seen. The heroes were sent spinning into a pile of rubbish sacks.
"Are you OK?" asked Gekko.
"Yes, but Romeo got all my feathers wet," frowned Owlette. "And he got away."

By the time Catboy came back,
he had missed the action.
"What happened?" he asked.
"You weren't here to help
us – again," said Owlette.
"That's what happened."

"VRROOM!"

Romeo zoomed into the street in the Cat-Car! He fired furballs at the PJ Masks. Quick as a flash, Catboy flipped his bike up into the air. "No one hurts my friends," he shouted.

"Super Cat Jump!"

Catboy sent the furballs bouncing back towards Romeo. He sped away.

Owlette and Gekko were super-impressed. "Amazing!" gasped Gekko. "You totally saved us."
Catboy had finally realised that his bike was just as cool as his Cat-Car.
"I'm glad you like it," said Owlette, "because our super vehicles are about to get crushed!"

Catboy had got another idea. It was time be a hero!
"I'm going to use my bike to beat Romeo.

Super Cat Speed!"

Catboy, Gekko and Owlette raced down the street.

The PJ Masks cycled into the park.
Romeo rushed towards his Lab.
"Stay back or I'll crush your
precious super vehicles
like tin cans!" he shouted.
Catboy cycled
up a stack of cars.

"POW!"

He knocked Romeo's
remote control out
of his hand.

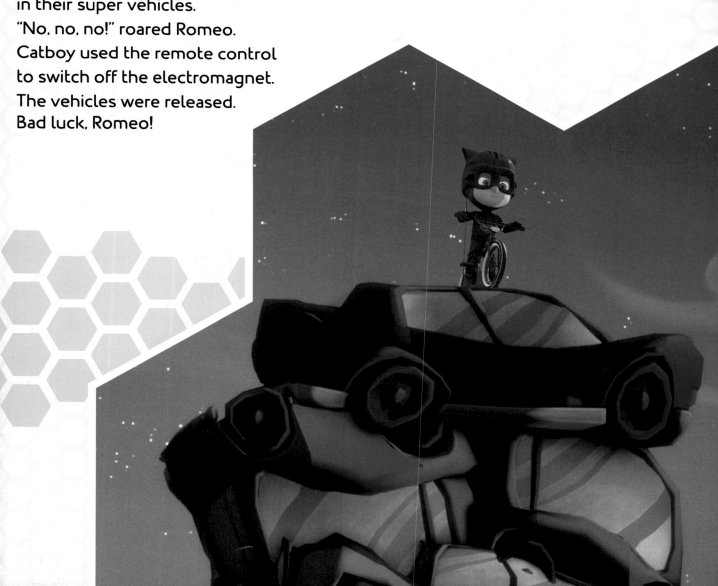

"PJ Masks, **GO!**"

Gekko and Owlette pedalled after Catboy. The heroes soared off the car stack, towards the electromagnet. One-by-one, they landed in their super vehicles.

"No, no, no!" roared Romeo.

Catboy used the remote control to switch off the electromagnet. The vehicles were released.

Bad luck, Romeo!

"Our bikes are so cool!" cheered Catboy.

"They helped us get our vehicles back," agreed Owlette.

"They won't help return these cars," joked Gekko.

"That will take Super Gekko Muscles!"

PJ MASKS ALL SHOUT HOORAY.
'CAUSE IN THE NIGHT, WE SAVED THE DAY!